TANGLED TALES

Meddling Underlins

Plib and her family have spent
years battling E.V.I.L. (Extremely
Vile Industries Limited) but now
their home is threatened. To save
them, Plib will have to work for the
enemy... but can she change things
for the better from the inside?

WRITTEN BY **LOU TRELEAVEN**
ILLUSTRATED BY **MARIO GUSHIKEN**

CHAPTER 1
Letters and Lies

Planet Slogg was becoming E.V.I.L. Not evil in small letters, but in giant, looming capital letters. E.V.I.L. stood for Extremely Vile Industries Limited, a company which made nearly everything on Planet Slogg, and pretty much everything in the rest of the Zolar System as well.

The things E.V.I.L. made ranged from houses and schools to washing powder and cat food, and all their products were evil in small letters too. E.V.I.L. made remote controls so small they would disappear down the back of the sofa so you had to buy a new one. They made washing machines that shrunk your clothes so you had to buy another washing machine and more clothes—all made by E.V.I.L. They manufactured things that broke down or ran out so you had to buy them again—and again.

It was very difficult not to buy E.V.I.L. products—they were everywhere. And so cheap that other companies had gone out of business trying to compete. From their headquarters on Planet Vile, the Vile family were gaining more and more power over the inhabitants of the Zolar System, and there was nothing anyone could do.

Or was there?

It was Plib's last day at school. She wasn't old enough to leave, but the school had become E.V.I.L. a couple of years ago. Since then, the desks had collapsed, the walls had crumbled and the playground was a death trap. The teachers had done their best, but it wasn't easy. All they could do was try to keep the pupils alive and hope they learned a few facts along the way. Now the whole building had caved in. Representatives of E.V.I.L. were standing outside as the pupils climbed out of the rubble, handing them leaflets on how to apply for jobs at E.V.I.L. factories.

"No minimum age! Earn yourself an E.V.I.L. loyalty card!"

Plib pretended not to hear, which was difficult on Planet Slogg where everyone had three ears and only two hands. "Thanks for nothing," she said, screwing up the leaflet and shoving it in her pocket. She wandered glumly home: past the E.V.I.L. hospital where the beds collapsed more than the patients, through the E.V.I.L. playground still awaiting renovation, and into the E.V.I.L. housing estate which was a permanent building site.

Today the estate was crowded with more cranes and bulldozers than ever. Plib dodged through them until she came to the best place on Planet Slogg: her house. Unlike most people, her family had resisted updating to an E.V.I.L. house when they had all looked so sparkling and new, before they started crumbling and people realised how evil E.V.I.L. really was.

"What's everyone doing home?" Plib asked.

Mum, Dad and her big sister Brox were sitting round the kitchen table with serious expressions.

"Plib, it's bad news," Mum said, waving a letter with an E.V.I.L. header. "They're demolishing this part of the estate."

"They can't do that!" Plib exclaimed.

"E.V.I.L. have bought the land and can do what they like," Dad said glumly. "Unless we have an E.V.I.L. loyalty card. But we're not giving in."

Plib looked to her sister. By day, Brox was a computer programmer. By night, she led the local resistance group fighting E.V.I.L. It didn't do much good, but they were all proud of her. Also, she had her third ear pierced which was the height of cool.

"It's clever," Brox said. "The Vile family won't rest until everything's E.V.I.L."

Mum sighed. "This is it, then. One of us will have to take an E.V.I.L. job to get the loyalty card. It's the only way to keep the house."

"No!" Plib groaned. "Mum, you love being a midwife. And Dad, you've always been so proud of your non-E.V.I.L. carpentry job. And Brox—you definitely can't, you're in the Resistance. So…"

Mum frowned. "I know what you're going to say Plib, but you're in school."

"*Was* in school. It fell down. Anyway, I can study by myself, in the evenings."

"You're a child!"

"E.V.I.L. employs children all the time."

"None of us *are* working for E.V.I.L., Plib," Mum said firmly. "We'll think of another way."

"But we can't lose our house!"

"Promise me you won't work for E.V.I.L. You know how we feel about them."

Plib crossed her fingers behind her back and tried not to look at Brox. "I promise."

CHAPTER 2
Sisters and Stilton

That evening, after Brox had left for her Resistance meeting, Plib slipped outside. Two crescent moons shone overhead, while a faint twinkle showed the position of Planet Vile, the captured asteroid that was home to the Vile family and the root of all E.V.I.L.

Planet Slogg's E.V.I.L. Head Office wasn't hard to find: the giant letters spelling out E.V.I.L. and threatening to fall on people's heads were a big clue. The squealing revolving door trapped Plib for ages before spitting her out into the shabbily decorated foyer.

"I'm here about a job," Plib said dizzily.

"Child labour, eh? Let's see." The man at the desk turned to his computer. "Name?"

"Plib, short for—"

"Here you go."

Plib looked at the E.V.I.L. loyalty card the man had handed to her. 'F.O.E. – Friend of E.V.I.L.'. It was that easy.

"Report to the Product Adjustment Centre at 6:00am tomorrow. Here's your ID badge."

"What about my family? They might lose their house."

"Address?"

"1061 Bobble Street."

The man pressed a few keys. "I've filed a request. Welcome to E.V.I.L., Miss Plib."

The next morning, the Zun was blasting

out its first garish beams as Plib walked to the Product Adjustment Centre, a large warehouse ten minutes from home. A bored woman scanned her ID badge and directed her onto the shop floor, yelling above the noise of machinery for someone called Maxod.

Maxod was tall and thin with long red hair in a ponytail. His two ears were on the left rather than the right which was less usual.

"New?" he said gloomily.

Plib nodded.

"It's pretty simple. E.V.I.L. make their products all over the Zolar System, then the ones for sale on Slogg come to places like this for hand-finishing by children. Our job is to make them even worse. You'll start on lunchboxes."

Plib picked up a thin plastic lunchbox decorated with a badly drawn cartoon character. "Looks pretty bad already."

"Wait till the mouldy cheese stuck in the corner is stinking out your house."

"But there isn't—" Plib began, before noticing a block of pungent Stilton.

Maxod handed her rubber gloves. "In a month they'll be buying another one. Just make sure you ram the cheese right into the cracks."

Twelve hours later, Plib had planted six hundred cheese timebombs and her shift was over. She staggered out with the other children into the double moonlit evening.

"Fun?" Maxod asked.

"Worst day of my life."

"You learn to switch off. Not that there's anything wrong with creating E.V.I.L. products. Long live E.V.I.L., that's what I say!"

The supervisor was walking through them, her presence like a bucketful of cold water. After a few more exchanges of "Long live E.V.I.L.!" the children scattered.

Maxod waved glumly. "See you at six tomorrow."

Another twelve-hour shift! All Plib wanted to do was sleep. Thank goodness her parents were out tonight, visiting a new non-E.V.I.L. restaurant before it closed down. She trudged home and stumbled into the kitchen.

"I covered for you this morning." Brox was nursing a cup of tea.

Plib grabbed and drained it in one motion. "I'd love to talk, but I haven't been to the toilet for twelve hours, so..."

"When were you going to tell me you'd got a job at E.V.I.L.?" Brox held up a black card with a silver F.O.E. on it. Oh poop. Plib had left her loyalty card at home.

"Er…"

"Talk, little sis."

"I couldn't have you all betraying your principles, could I?"

"I don't know whether to shout at you or hug you, Plib."

"While you decide, I'm going to the toilet."

When Plib returned, Brox had produced more tea and a plate of biscuits.

"I should tell Mum and Dad, but I won't," she said. "*If* you do something for me."

"Of course," Plib said. "Sisters forever." It was something they always said to each other, at least when they weren't arguing.

Brox's eyes gleamed. "I'm fed up with being a victim. With you in there, the Resistance can inflict damage where it really hurts. It's time to fight back. Together."

CHAPTER 3

Secrets and Supervisors

Plib's first week at the Product Adjustment Centre was exhausting, but it was worth it when her parents received a letter saying their house wasn't going to be demolished after all.

"I don't understand it," Dad said. "But I'm not complaining."

"It's probably a mistake," Mum said. "Nothing nice like this ever happens to us. Talking of which, how's your job at the genetically-modified animal shelter going, Plib?"

"Great!" Plib lied. "I love looking after the hamsterdiles."

It was horrible deceiving the people she loved, but at least they hadn't lost their home.

One evening, Plib flopped down on the sofa, even more tired than usual and hoping cheese wasn't on the dinner menu. "I'm back!"

"Actually, you're not." Brox ushered her out of the door. "It's time you met the Resistance. Let me just blindfold you so you don't give away our location." Brox laughed at Plib's unimpressed face. "Only joking. We meet in the old library. I've covered things with Mum and Dad."

The library had been closed by E.V.I.L. four years ago. The empty shelves looked down sadly as Plib and Brox walked to a shabby meeting room with a broken window.

Plib had never met the other members of

the Resistance. Brox hadn't shared this part of her life with her before. She peered around in the gloom. "Where is everyone?"

"Hmm, seems pretty quiet tonight. Never mind. Plib, it's time for you to start recruiting others. We need to find out who's on our side."

"I'll try," Plib said. "Also, I've been secretly improving some of the products instead of breaking them."

"That sounds dangerous. But it could be a way to unite the rebels. Just don't get caught and keep all three ears to the ground."

The next day, Plib felt jittery. It would be a huge risk identifying who was prepared to stand up to E.V.I.L. Her only comfort was that it was Brox giving her instructions. Brox always knew the best thing to do.

"Good morning!" Plib called out as usual as she passed the front desk.

"Never going to respond, ever," the sour supervisor grunted. "Oh wait. Plob, Plub, whatever. Here's a new employee. I'm putting him on lunchboxes. You're now on toasters. Make sure the bread pops in people's faces."

A small, pale boy with greasy hair looked at Plib nervously. "Hi Plub, I'm O... liver."

Plib gave him a reassuring smile. She knew exactly how he felt. "It's Plib. Sorry you've got to work here, Oliver, but you'll soon get used to the long hours, boring work and terrible pay. I'll show you around."

What luck! This was the perfect opportunity for visiting the other workspaces and seeing who else she might recruit to her cause. Though as most of them chanted "Long live E.V.I.L.!" as soon as she approached, the answer was probably not many. Nobody wanted to risk losing their job.

"And this is you," she said, arriving back at lunchboxes. "Just shove the cheese in these cracks so they slowly start to stink. You'll get used to the pong."

"Fine," Oliver said with a shrug.

He looked thoroughly fed up. Plib put a comforting hand on his shoulder. "It'll be okay. I know it all seems bleak and pointless, but you have to have hope."

He twisted round and stared at her.

"But... long live E.V.I.L., right?" she added.

"Yeah," he mumbled. "Right."

Later into her shift, Maxod nodded at her. "That new kid looks crushed already," he whispered as Plib wrestled with a toaster. "Hey, what are you doing?"

Plib decided to take a chance. "I'm improving the toaster so it works properly."

Maxod stared at her. "A few of us do that sometimes too. Lunch with us today?"

"I should stick with Oliver, cheer him up. He just stares out of the window. I don't think he's used up a single block of cheese yet."

"Sounds promising. Bring him too."

CHAPTER 4

Cupboards and Confidences

"Hello? Brox?" Plib called as she entered the library meeting room that evening.

Brox was huddled over a screen with her back to Plib. "I have to go," Plib heard her say as she switched the screen off.

"Isn't anyone coming tonight either?" Plib asked.

Brox shrugged. "Er... I expect they're all engaged in top secret Resistance activities, like I've just been. Welcome to the meeting. Tell me what you know."

"Well, I've started having lunch with a

few people who might be sympathetic to our cause. Maxod, Florn and Arjax are all trying to mend things when they can. And there's a new boy we're sussing out too."

"Good. Now on to the plan. We need you to get access to the supervisor's computer. I've created a virus that will corrupt the warehouse's system."

"Wow."

"Don't 'wow' too soon. It might not work."

"But how do I get into the supervisor's office without her seeing?"

"With the help of your new friends, that's how."

Plib couldn't help yearning for the old days when all she had to do was handle cheese. Now she had to lead a group of rebels in a deadly plot. Would they even agree?

@

At lunchtime the next day, Plib spread the word and they all squeezed into a cupboard.

"You too, Oliver."

The new boy had taken to following her around like a sad puppy. Sometimes it felt like she really was working at the animal shelter.

"Do we have to have lunch in here?" Florn asked, freeing her dark braids from a nest of cables.

"Plib asked me to find a place we could meet in secret," Maxod said, folding himself smaller so Arjax could get in.

It was time to come clean. Sort of. "I have a... um... friend in the Resistance." Plib kept her voice low. "She programs computers and she has a virus."

"Is it the Splurts?" Arjax asked, pushing up his glasses. "I've heard that is really nasty."

"A *computer* virus," Plib explained. "It could bring the whole warehouse to a halt."

"Why?" Arjax asked.

"Because someone has to stand up to E.V.I.L. Right?"

There was a brief silence as everyone absorbed the enormity of what Plib was saying. Of course, they would refuse. Why risk their loyalty cards? Their families? They would be quite right to report her too. Plib's knees shook. Rumour had it that when an E.V.I.L. employee got fired, they got really fired. Out of a cannon. It was probably just a silly story, but she didn't want to find out.

"This is just one tiny workplace," Arjax said. "It won't make any difference. E.V.I.L. is on every planet in the Zolar System!"

"It will make a difference to us," Plib said, realising that she believed what she was saying.

Florn nodded. "I'm sick of making life worse for people. Finally, we can do something!"

"Shh, they'll hear us!" Maxod said. "But I agree. I had to work here to get an E.V.I.L. loyalty card so my dad could get his disability benefits. It's not right. Arjax?"

"I too am sick of doing nothing," Arjax admitted. "You're right, let's fight E.V.I.L. and the Vile family! But what about him?"

Everyone looked at Oliver. The new boy

was sweating and fidgety. Had she misjudged him? Was he the sort to tell?

"You can leave now and not be a part of this," she told him.

Oliver looked like he was attempting to swallow a big dose of courage. "I'm in."

"Brilliant!" Florn said. "It's about time that old witch up there on Planet Vile got what's coming to her."

Oliver choked and Plib patted him on the back. "I hear her grandson's going to take over the company one day," he said between coughs.

"He's just as bad," Arjax said. "Apparently Mrs Vile's son was alright. Until his mum slammed him into her own private dungeon."

"Lovely family," Florn said brightly. "Well, looks like we're all with you, Plib. But we haven't thought of the most important thing—a name."

There was a murmur of excitement as everyone tried to think of a better name than anyone else.

"How about Gang of Organised Dissenters, or **G.O.O.D.?**" Maxod suggested.

This had gone so much better than Plib had expected. "Let's get some lunch—that stale bread and watery soup won't eat itself," she announced with relief.

Everyone spilled out of the cupboard. Oliver looked slightly green.

"Are you alright?" Plib asked.

"I'm fine," the new boy mumbled, holding his ear as he hurried away.

Maxod looked after him doubtfully. "Do you think we can trust him?"

"I hope so," Plib mused. "If not, it's too late now."

CHAPTER 5
Cereals and Celebrities

Plib tried to sleep but her brain couldn't remember how. She was about to do something illegal. She told herself it was for a good reason. E.V.I.L. had to be stopped, didn't it?

They had been over the plan, and everyone had their part to play. Oliver was off sick, but when he came back he would be working on removing the bounce from bouncy balls and could knock a big box of them all over the warehouse. The others would chase them, causing chaos and drawing the supervisor out of her office so Plib could get in.

As Plib arrived on The Day, Florn gave her a nervy smile. Arjax winked. Even Maxod had a spring in his step. But Oliver wasn't back.

"He's left," the supervisor yawned when Plib and Maxod asked. "And don't ask me why 'cause I'm not interested."

Plib and Maxod exchanged despairing looks. Without Oliver, they would have to rethink the plan. And someone else was going to be even less impressed: Brox.

But, to Plib's surprise, Brox wasn't annoyed at all. It wasn't until Saturday morning—when the sisters had breakfast together while their parents had a lie in—that they had a chance to talk.

"These aren't Fudgy Flakes!" Plib exclaimed. "And the box is half empty. It's not an E.V.I.L. cereal, is it?"

Brox shrugged. "It was that or nothing, okay?"

Plib poured the scrawny hoops into her bowl. "Look, we'll have to change the plan. Oliver has disappeared. I'm worried about him."

"Doesn't matter." Brox helped herself to the rest of the hoops. "There are bigger fish to fry."

"Fish? I only wanted cereal."

Brox wasn't listening. "Why should the Vile family control our lives? Who put them in charge?" She laid down her spoon. "I'm sorry to get you involved. I really am. But this new plan is too good a chance to miss."

Brox patted Plib on the shoulder as she left. Plib stared after her. What was Brox up to now?

BING BONG!

Normally the speakers at the Product Adjustment Centre blasted out demotivating messages telling people to ignore the stars and stay in the gutter. Today was different.

"Attention, workers," droned the supervisor. "E.V.I.L. will shortly be celebrating their fiftieth anniversary. Whoopee. And we have been given tickets to reward our star workers. Since you're all useless, the completely random people who will attend this lavish, celebrity-studded event of the century on Planet Vile are... pause for ten seconds... Florn, Arjax, Maxod and Plib."

The rest of the warehouse groaned and went back to work, prickling with jealousy.

No one wanted anything more to do with E.V.I.L. than they had to, but how often did the chance to attend a 'lavish, celebrity-studded event of the century' come along? Never: that was how often.

"They know!" Plib burst out as they gathered outside at the end of the shift.

"Know what?" Florn asked. "Hey, what's everyone going to wear?"

The group erupted in a babble of excitement.

"Stop!" Plib cried. "We're not actually going, are we?"

"Plib, I've never left the city," Maxod said. "We'll be flying there in a spaceship, doing things we've never done before—"

"Like the cosmic conga!" Florn interrupted.

"I wonder if there'll be a chocolate fountain?" Arjax pondered.

⑥

"...And that's all they were worried about!" Plib complained to Brox, who was waiting for her when she got home. "It was like we'd never made our rebel alliance at all."

"Good," Brox said, "because the Resistance has finalised the plan. Come on or we'll be late."

"Can't you just tell me now?"

"Alright. We want you to go to Planet Vile. Forget trying to scramble the warehouse's computer. You can infect the inner workings of E.V.I.L. itself!"

"Me? Go to Planet Vile? But that's where E.V.I.L. is based. It's where the Vile family lives."

"That's the point! You could put a stop to everything."

"I'd like to help but... it's terrifying." Plib

sunk into a chair.

Brox crouched in front of her. "Would it help if I went with you?"

"Could you?"

"Who else is going to help you crack the code? Sisters forever?"

"Sisters forever."

CHAPTER 6

Rockets and Resistance

Not for the first time, Plib wondered how she had got caught up in all this. If only she was back at school. If only it hadn't been taken over by E.V.I.L. But it had, and E.V.I.L. had designed the school to fail so no one would leave with the skills they needed to fight it.

She *had* to act, for all those who couldn't. She just wished she wasn't dragging the others along but she couldn't persuade them out of it.

Brox gave Plib a special jacket with a pocket that made the contents invisible to security checks. "Inside here is the USB stick with the virus," she explained.

"Wow, where did you get this?" Plib asked, marvelling at the quality.

"Never mind that," Brox snapped. "Locate the main computer, turn it on and plug the stick into the USB slot. The virus should do the rest. All of us wish you the best of luck."

"Thank you. All of you. And if I'm not lucky?"

"You'll be fired."

"Could be worse."

"No, I mean fired out of a giant space cannon. But you won't fail. I'll make sure of that."

⊚

The night of the party, Plib gave her parents a special hug before leaving.

Dad smiled. "I'm not complaining, but what was that for?"

35

"Nothing. Just—I love you."

"We love you too," Mum said. "You look nice by the way. Good luck with the rhinocerabbits!"

It was Plib's first time in space. Like most Sloggers she had never left her home planet, even though there was a whole Zolar System to explore. Space travel was expensive and mostly for VIPs. As the shuttle pulled away, she wondered if she'd ever see Planet Slogg again. Maybe she would get a good view from the space cannon before she exploded into tiny pieces.

She tucked Brox's new jacket around her old dress. It wasn't easy to glam up when clothes were made by E.V.I.L. Opposite her, Maxod was wearing a too-small suit that had once been silver. He gave her a thumbs up and a few disco arm moves, knocking Florn in the face.

"Ow! Now you've ruined my hair," Florn complained.

"You look lovely," Plib reassured her.

Florn repositioned a hairclip above her double right ears. "Still think we're heading to our doom?"

"Yep."

"Does this say 'doom' to you?" Maxod asked, flicking out the hologrammatic invite with little black 50s shooting off it in sparks.

"There it is!" Arjax cried, pointing out of the window. The knobbly lump of captured asteroid that was Planet Vile hung forebodingly in view. "Let's get ready to **PARTAAAAAY!"**

As they zoomed closer, metal towers spiked upwards. The planetary surface was bare and rocky where it wasn't covered with roads and landing strips. And everything looked cold and dark—they were much further away from the Zun here.

"What's that?" Florn asked, pointing at a big tube aimed at the sky.

"That must be the giant space cannon, for..." Plib stopped. If they were all going to die anyway, they might as well be happy a bit longer. "For firing confetti into the air."

"Aw!" everyone said, delighted.

Plib shivered as the asteroid came closer. She had to get to that computer—and fast.

As they approached, the ground slid open and the shuttle touched down in an underground hangar. Plib's group were hurried into a lift which took them up to a foyer leading into a huge hall. Black and silver banners declared 'Fifty Years of E.V.I.L.' and 'Congratulations On Your Horrible

Achievement!' Before all that was a line of tough-looking security guards. Plib walked towards them, her heart hammering. Would the USB stick be discovered? Would she be seeing the inside of that cannon for herself?

"Welcome to the T.O.E., miss," said a black-clad figure with a hood, ushering her to one side.

"Toe?"

"Tower of E.V.I.L. May I scan your ID?"

The voice was familiar. "Brox? Is that you?"

"Sshh." Brox scanned Plib's badge, then patted her down. "All clear. Enjoy the E.V.I.L. occasion."

"Brox?" Plib whispered. "Will you help me rescue the others, if... if something goes wrong?"

Brox jerked her head to the security guards. "See that lot? They're with me."

Wow, the Resistance had finally turned up! Suddenly Plib felt a lot better. Whispering a final 'sisters forever', she went into the hall and accepted a fancy drink from a waiter while the others completed their security checks.

The room was bustling with special guests in expensive outfits, sipping sparkling drinks and wandering around the displays of E.V.I.L.'s bestselling products: the oversensitive smoke alarm, the quick-popping balloon, and the instantly unfashionable mobile phone. She also spotted some celebrities, enclosed in transparent plastic tubes to protect them from the public. The rest were like Plib: workers in shabby clothes, awestruck and gripping their special tickets. The centre of the room was dominated by a model of the Zolar System. Most of the planets were covered with letter Vs.

"Each one of those Vs represents an E.V.I.L. business," a boy's voice was explaining to a group of important-looking people. "So, as you can see, E.V.I.L. will soon be taking over the entire..." The voice died away as the speaker's eyes met Plib's.

"Oliver?" she gasped.

Oliver's hair was greased back and he wore a long cloak over a pinstriped suit. Plib was about to ask if he had come in fancy dress and how he had disguised his third ear when there was a sudden hush as a thin, elderly woman in a shimmering, dark suit marched up.

"I want you on stage with me, Otis."

"But—"

"But? But? Are you a goat, Otis? Now!" She stalked off again and Plib felt everyone in the room relax.

"Right behind you, Grandmother!" Otis called after her.

Plib stepped back in horror. "You're Otis Vile?"

"It was the two ears that gave me away, wasn't it?"

"No, it was the 'living on Planet Vile and calling Mrs Vile grandmother' that gave you away. How could you deceive us?"

"I was undercover. I'm sorry—"

"Sorry!?" Suddenly Plib understood everything. "You betrayed us, didn't you? That's why we were invited here."

"No! I mean, yes, but there was a reason."

"I don't want anything to do with you."

Otis leaned in and spoke into her ear. "Listen. 1, 2, 3, 4 is the passcode for my grandmother's computer. I know you can do something. Your friends need to help too. Please, Plib—"

"OTIIIIIIIIS!"

Mrs Vile's scream filled the hall.

"I have to go. Her office is on Floor 66. Hurry!"

CHAPTER 7
Speeches and Cybercrime

Oliver was Otis Vile.

Otis was part of E.V.I.L.

But Otis had asked her to get into the computer and destroy E.V.I.L.! Was it all a trick?

She tuned into Mrs Vile's speech. "But despite my efforts, there are still some 'nice' people around who want to make the world a better place. I'm going to fire them tonight. Literally. The giant cannon has been prepared and we will shortly be ejecting fifty specially selected workers into the vacuum of space."

Oh poop. Maybe Otis's plan was worth chancing after all.

"This way!" Plib hissed, grabbing Maxod and the others.

The four of them stumbled out into the foyer.

"What did you do that for? The buffet's about to open!" Arjax complained.

"Yes, and you know what else is about to open? The jaws of death. Didn't you hear what she said about fifty workers being fired into space? That includes us!"

"We haven't done the cosmic conga yet!" Florn objected.

Plib opened the door a crack. Mrs Vile was still talking. And as a three-eared species, it wasn't difficult for them to hear.

"...Anybody who has received one of these special invites will be cannon fodder. Security, seize them!"

Maxod fished out the hologrammatic invitation and threw it to the floor. "Yikes!"

"To Floor 66!" Plib commanded.

"What about the security guards over there?" Arjax asked.

"That's alright, they're Resistance." Plib raised her voice. "Anyone seen Brox?"

The guards reached for their weapons.

"Double poop, they're not Resistance after all. To the lift! **RUUUUUUUUUN!**"

Maxod got there first and yanked them in.

"Top floor," Plib panted. "Oh, I wish Brox was here. She should be doing this, not me."

She explained to the others about Otis as the lift zoomed upwards. Hopefully it wasn't made by E.V.I.L., or it would break down and they would be stuffed.

"Are we really going to be fired out of a cannon?" Arjax asked.

"Not if I can help it," Plib assured him. "Here we are: Floor 66."

They ran out and pushed open the only door.

"Wow." The biggest desk Plib had ever seen sat in front of the biggest window she had ever seen. Statues stood about scowling and a portrait showed Mrs Vile receiving the 'Shoddiest Goods Award' for her invention of the collapsing dining chair. "Yep, this is her office. Barricade the door, Maxod! I need to input some numbers, but where?"

As Maxod pushed the heavy desk against the door, Arjax shouted for Plib. Under where the desk had been was a rug with Mrs Vile's face woven into it, and under that Arjax had found four paving-slab-sized buttons.

"I get it! We need to stand on the numbers. Maxod, over here on number one!" Plib called.

"Three's my favourite number," Arjax said,

bagging it.

"Mine too!" Florn protested.

"We're wasting time!" Plib jumped onto four. A section of the wall rose revealing a screen with an option to **'ENTER E.V.I.L.'**

"Done it! I've just got to press the screen and..." Plib stepped off her number and the screen went black and began to disappear again. "Triple poop, I can't reach! Everyone back on their buttons."

"Maybe Maxod can lie across them," Florn suggested.

But Maxod wasn't heavy enough.

"It's no good, we need a fifth person to work the screen," Plib said, groaning with frustration.

They looked at each other, stumped. Then there was a bang and a grinding sound as the door was forced open.

"You found the access panel!" Otis exclaimed.

"Thanks for coming, everyone. Help me overpower this goon, will you?"

Behind Otis was a security guard, seemingly stunned to find himself in Mrs Vile's office. They all jumped on him and soon he was safely tied up with computer cables.

"The boss is going to kill me!" he moaned.

Otis had a smile on his face. It suited him. "Thanks. For trusting me, I mean," he said.

"Thanks for trusting *us!*" Plib grinned. "G.O.O.D. is back! Everyone, get on those buttons. Otis, we need you."

Plib, Maxod, Florn and Arjax took their places and Otis ran to the screen to press **'ENTER E.V.I.L.'**

The words made Plib shiver. Was *she* doing evil? But Brox had told her to do it. And Brox had devoted herself to resisting E.V.I.L. Surely she could be trusted to choose the right action?

"Plib? Have you still got the computer virus?"

Plib reached into her pocket. There was nothing there. And suddenly she wondered if it had ever been there. There were a million questions she wanted to ask Brox, but now wasn't the time.

"It's not here. I don't understand. My sister should be here helping, but..."

"Don't worry, I've got a better idea. I'll start by disabling the cannon." Otis scrolled through a huge menu, then pressed some keys. From far away there came a distant *pfffffffsss* and a groan of disappointment. Florn and Arjax broke into a celebratory dance.

"Stay on those buttons!" Otis warned them. "This is just the beginning."

Plib watched Otis in amazement. He was like a different person.

"What else can you get into?" she asked.

"Cut the power?" Florn suggested.

Otis scrolled frantically. "Good idea—if I cut it to the lower floors my dad will be able to escape from the dungeons. Done!"

"If your dad's free, will he be able to take over the company?" Plib asked.

"He's not evil enough for E.V.I.L., and neither am I. I'll do as much damage as I can, then Dad and I will try to escape somewhere."

Plib could think of only one place as home. "Come to Planet Slogg. It's zunny. And you can stay with us."

"My grandmother won't be very happy with you."

"She won't be happy with me anyway after what we've done. And we don't even know how we're going to escape so..."

Otis grinned. "I can fix that." He pressed

some more keys. "Right, the S.H.O.E. is ready for kick-off. I'll explain later," he added, seeing Plib's puzzled face. "Okay, anything else we can do?"

"Ooh, ooh, ooh!" Arjax cried. "We should change their name! From E.V.I.L. to…"

Everybody thought hard to come up with the best name first.

"The Notable Industrial Company of Evil— or **N.I.C.E.!**" Maxod suggested.

There was a begrudging murmur of approval. Maxod had done it again.

"You could have given me a few more seconds," Arjax complained.

"Brilliant!" Otis said, and he actually laughed as he inputted the change. "Now, how can we make E.V.I.L. more N.I.C.E.? Let's start with working conditions. Free ice cream on Fridays, anyone?"

After a joyous few minutes making the Product Alignment Centre plus all the other E.V.I.L. workplaces in the Zolar System the nicest ever, Otis reminded them they'd better get out of there.

"A thought," Maxod said. "What's to stop Mrs Vile undoing everything?"

"Hmm. Well, she hasn't got four friends, and the security guards don't come up here. I wonder how *she* unlocks the computer?"

"Does it matter? Let's get out of here before she does!" Florn said.

The guard was snoring. Plib tucked a cushion under his head while the others replaced the furniture.

"Those statues are truly awful!" Florn remarked.

Otis didn't seem to mind Florn's comment. "That's it! She must use the statues to weigh

down the buttons! But what can we do about them?"

It was then that Plib had her first ever, and last ever, evil thought. "Well," she said, looking out of the window with a mischievous smile. "It's a very long way down..."

As they came out of the office to summon the lift, brushing bits of broken statue off themselves, a man who looked like an Otis who had been aged, stretched, and fallen in a skip limped towards them wearing a Cosmic Death Lords t-shirt.

"Everyone, this is my dad," Otis said proudly.

Mr Vile waved. "Pleased to meet you. Did you hear the one about—"

"Sorry, no time for dad jokes," Otis said. "Can we get to the S.H.O.E.?"

"We can try. Are these your friends?"

Otis looked at them uncertainly. "Yyyyes?"

"Of course we are!" Plib said, stepping forward. "Good to meet you, Mr Vile. You're very welcome to come back to Planet Slogg with us."

"Where Otis goes, I go," Otis's dad said. "But first I quite fancy a ride in this device."

He pressed the button to call the lift. The doors slid open and a hooded figure stepped out.

"There you are, my little rebels."

CHAPTER 8

Upsets and Uprisings

It was Brox. Plib wanted to rush up and hug her, but her sister seemed steely and remote.

"We're taking the S.H.O.E. and you can't stop us," Otis burst out.

"Stop us? She's coming with us!" Plib cried.

Brox shook her head. "I've got a job to do here. Something I've been working towards for a long time."

"You were planning to take over all along," Otis exclaimed.

Plib was confused. Brox wasn't coming?

Brox pressed the lift button and stood

aside as the doors slid open again. "One day I hope you'll understand. Now go on. Hurry!"

The lift doors closed on them, and they hurtled downwards. Plib gulped back tears. Why was Brox staying? And why hadn't she given Plib the USB stick? She wiped her eyes on the sleeve of her jacket—Brox's jacket. The important thing now was to escape. She could think about it all later when—if—they got away.

In the hangar, an angular space shuttle waited, its lights blinking. In the doorway stood Mrs Vile and a muscular security guard. Poop city.

"How lovely," Mrs Vile sneered. "My ex-family and some meddling underlings, trying to get away."

"Hello Mother," Otis's dad said. "Do you know why mother kangaroos hate rainy days?

Because the kids have to play inside!"

"I see you haven't changed, Ernold," Mrs Vile remarked icily. "Still acting like a pathetic teenager."

Mr Vile's face lit up. "A pathetic teenager who once built his own spaceship! Come on, kids, let's take the cool car. This way!"

Otis's dad half ran, half hobbled over to a corner of the hanger. With a flush of pride, he pulled away a tarpaulin, revealing a small, clunky, cobbled-together space pod.

"I knocked this up when I was a youngster. It may not be working after all these years, but..."

Plib was prepared to take the chance. She bundled in with the others as Mr Vile pressed some buttons. Amazingly, the homemade pod lifted into the air as Mrs Vile shook her fist at them and appeared to shout at her crew.

As they catapulted away from Planet Vile in a streak of blue smoke, Mr Vile connected his enormous speakers to the output of the S.H.O.E., where Mrs Vile was raging at her crew.

"Sorry but there's been a supply chain issue, Mrs Vile. We've, um, we've been using E.V.I.L. parts for months now," the terrified pilot was explaining.

"You're telling me we're using our *own* parts? Then this whole spaceship is a pile of junk! *Aaarrrrrgggggggghhhhhhh!*"

Everyone around Plib clapped and cheered as the S.H.O.E. failed to take off and began to fall apart, and Mr Vile put his favourite heavy metal track on the speakers to celebrate.

"Bye Brox," Plib whispered as they whizzed away into space.

※

"Plib!" Mum and Dad embraced her tightly at the front door. It was so good to see them and to feel the zunlight on her face.

"We were so worried about you," Dad said.

"Yes, we heard you'd started working for E.V.I.L.," Mum added.

Plib hugged them back. "It's worse than that. I've brought home two members of the Vile family. Please can they stay with us, just until they've worked out how to live without E.V.I.L.?"

"They can have Brox's room," Mum decided as everyone was introduced. "Apparently she's got a promotion at work and won't be home for a while. Her room's tiny though. Will it be alright?"

As Plib frowned, Otis's dad beamed. "Sounds like a five-star hotel to me."

@

Plib decided to stay at the Product Adjustment Centre. Thanks to the changes they had made, it was a very different place. Everyone now improved products rather than ruining them, and they even got to create their own: Maxod's cheese scone maker was very popular. Each worker also had proper holidays, shorter shifts and the day off for their birthday. The loyalty card scheme ended. And, at Otis's insistence, there was always cake.

Otis came back too while his father recovered, and together he and Plib worked on a new type of sandwich toaster that printed messages of freedom and positivity onto the bread.

"I can't stay forever," Otis told her. "Grandmother has issued a statement: she's disowned us and managed to change the name of the company back to E.V.I.L. I need to carry on the fight before she undoes all the other good work."

"But you can't go back to Planet Vile!" Plib protested, engraving a heart onto a sandwich toaster plate.

"I can if I'm undercover." Otis grinned. "I'll pretend to be from Planet Slogg. I've got quite fond of the ear, and your mum's offered to get me an extra bio-arm from the hospital's Spare Appendages Department."

Plib's thoughts turned, as they often did, to Brox. Was the plan more complex than she'd thought, or had Brox been playing a different game all along? "Will you find out what's happened to my sister?" she asked, a lump in her throat.

"I'll try, I promise. And I'm determined to find out who Number 2 is and what she's up to. Number 2 is a mystery."

"And *I* promise to continue the fight here. I'm going to take over the Resistance and drum up some members. We'll start by campaigning to reopen the library. One day, Planet Slogg is going to be a happy place again."

As Plib waved Otis off on the shuttle to Planet Vile soon after, she knew this was just the beginning. But maybe, one day, it would be the beginning of the end of E.V.I.L.

CHAPTER 1

Cakes and Computers

"Happy birthday to you!" Otis sang, joining in with everyone around him. Seeing all the smiling faces gave him a strange fluttering in his heart. Was this the thing he had heard about called 'happiness'?

Whatever it was, it didn't last.

"What in the name of E.V.I.L. is going on here?" demanded a thin, sour-faced woman in a grey

TANGLED TALES

UnderCover Overlord

Otis Vile is set to take over his
dastardly grandmother's even more
dastardly galactic corporation, E.V.I.L.
(Extremely Vile Industries Limited).
Only first he must go undercover in
their factories to root out anyone
'nice' once and for all. But is that all
Otis will find along the way?

To Greg, the undercover overlord of book titles!

WRITTEN BY **LOU TRELEAVEN**

C334971213

business suit. "And what is that?"

"It-it-it's my birthday," Ruby from I.T. stuttered, "and that's a cake."

"A what?"

"A cake, Mrs Vile. A birthday cake."

"'Birthday' and 'cake' are not in my vocabulary. And you are no longer my employee. Whose idea was this?" Mrs Vile demanded, as Ruby tearfully packed up her belongings.

"Er... mine," a man said, putting up one of his three hands. Everyone who worked on Planet Vile came from different parts of the Zolar System and it was common to see people with two noses or four legs—although you usually heard Four-Legged Fred coming before you saw him.

"No, it was all of us," the woman next to him said. Everybody nodded, especially a

person with two heads.

"How noble," Mrs Vile said. "And how utterly un-E.V.I.L. You are all dismissed."

"But we're the I.T. department," said the man. "How are you going to run E.V.I.L.'s computer system?"

"By not buying cakes!" Mrs Vile shrieked. "And not having birthdays. Birthdays and cakes are banned! And anything else to do with birthdays. Otis?" She clicked her fingers at him.

Otis jumped. "Er, balloons? Presents?" He had heard of such things, even though he'd never had them himself.

"Those are banned too. From now on, I will control the computer system. As for you..." Mrs Vile turned her furious gaze on Otis. "Come!"

Otis bit his lip. "Yes, Grandmother."

Planet Vile was a tamed asteroid and headquarters of Extremely Vile Industries Limited, or E.V.I.L. It was also the home of the Vile family: Otis Vile and, most importantly, his grandmother. The main building, the Tower of E.V.I.L. or T.O.E., was a soaring office block decorated in black and chrome to look menacing to visitors. Mrs Vile's office was the most menacing of all. The walls were black, her desk shiny and vast, and life-size statues of herself stood about, looking annoyed.

"What were you doing?" she demanded.

"Pardon?" As usual, Otis wished he could get closer to his grandmother, but her desk was nearly always between them.

"I said, what were you doing in the I.T. department when you are supposed to be in here with me training to be the future Overlord of E.V.I.L.?"

"I was invited to the... to the..."

"I'll allow you to say it just this once."

"Party."

"And did you think that was appropriate? Employees having fun? Laughter? Singing?" The words dripped from Mrs Vile's mouth like poison.

"It made me feel funny inside," Otis explained. "Like honey."

"Honey." Mrs Vile looked troubled. "These feelings you are having must stop, Otis. Only happiness makes you 'feel funny'. And happiness has no place in this family or this company. Understood?"

Otis had always understood. He had been brought up by his grandmother, except for the very first part of his life when his father had still been alive. For two wonderful, amazing years he had experienced love. And

then it had been taken away.

"I hope you're thinking evil thoughts, Otis."

"Yes, Grandmother."

"What do you think you've been doing for the last ten years? You are here to be trained in E.V.I.L., to inherit the company and, one day, become the Overlord of our empire. Do you know what special event is coming up?"

Otis was almost too afraid to speak. "Fifty years of E.V.I.L."

"Fifty years since I started making useless products that have to be bought over and over again! And I intend to mark the occasion. No singing, no cake. No, I just want every one of my employees to be completely evil, just like our products, in time for the anniversary." Mrs Vile paused for effect, but Otis didn't know what to say so she carried on. "And *you* will help."

This time Otis did respond. "How?"

"You will visit the main factories on each planet, look for signs of good, and report back to Number 2 so the culprits can be dealt with. Also look for evidence of the Resistance—a group who are actively opposing E.V.I.L. Apparently, we're causing poverty around the Zolar System. Boo hoo." Mrs Vile frowned. "Do you not like this plan?"

"Yes, of course—but what if people find out it's me...?"

"You will have a new identity. The Undercover Overlord."

"Yes, Grandmother," Otis said dutifully.

"And if that doesn't make you evil, nothing will," Mrs Vile added under her breath.

CHAPTER 2

Bracelets and Building Sites

"Well, well, well. I hardly recognise you," Mrs Vile crowed.

"And that's... good?" Otis asked. It felt odd wearing sports clothes instead of a suit—like he hadn't got dressed properly. Even at night he wore suit-patterned pyjamas. Grandmother insisted on office wear at all times.

"Of course it's good! Do you want to be recognised as the trainee Overlord of E.V.I.L.?"

"Yes. I mean, no."

Mrs Vile came closer to Otis than she had ever come before. "Do you understand

your mission?"

"To travel round the Zolar System pretending to be a new employee and report back on anyone who isn't evil."

"Report back to Number 2, Otis. I don't want to hear your bleating little voice the whole time you're away."

Mrs Vile pressed a button on her bracelet and a screen fizzled into life on the nearest wall.

"Number 2 here. I'm listening."

Otis stared at Number 2 but, as usual, the dark hooded cloak she always wore obscured her identity.

"Just a test, Number 2." Mrs Vile pressed the button again and the screen fizzled out. "It's time for you to leave the T.O.E. Ready the S.H.O.E.!" she commanded.

Outside, the judder of the Vile family's ancient space shuttle of E.V.I.L., or S.H.O.E., started up.

"Goodbye, Grandmother," Otis said, picking up his case.

"Wait." Mrs Vile bent down in front of him and held out her bracelet. Otis stared at the beautiful silver band. Could it be that Grandmother cared for him after all?

"I'll wear it and think of you," he promised.

"No you won't! **YUCK!** You'll use it to communicate with Number 2." Mrs Vile

stood up with a sigh. "I despair of you, Otis. This is your last chance. If you don't complete this task to my satisfaction, you are no longer my grandson."

Otis put the bracelet on his wrist. How stupid he was. Of course she didn't care for him. She only cared about E.V.I.L.

But as the shuttle left Planet Vile for the jewelled vastness of space, Otis touched the bracelet gently. For a moment, he had experienced what it might be like to be loved. If he could please his grandmother and complete this task, maybe things would change. She could never love him—that wasn't in her nature—but she could, surely, be proud of him. He had to get in touch with his evil side. He was a Vile, after all.

A small transfer pod took Otis and a bodyguard down to the capital of Planet Drizz. This was where the first of E.V.I.L.'s factories had been built, two generations ago. Otis marvelled at the sturdy old building, erected before the Vile family started creating things not to last.

"Welcome to your local E.V.I.L. head office," said the woman on the front desk with a large false smile.

The bodyguard, posing as Otis's father, explained he had come to enrol his son as a child labourer. Both he and Otis were wearing a pair of false eyebrows halfway up their foreheads so they would fit in on Drizz.

"Everyone's welcome to work until you drop for the sake of E.V.I.L. He can go and work on the roads if he likes. The Land Eater

is just leaving now."

Otis saw with horror that a huge, dirty vehicle on caterpillar tracks was grinding up outside. "But—"

Was that a smirk on his bodyguard's face? "Bye, 'son'. See you in twelve hours."

Fuming, Otis stomped off to the vehicle. He would report that double-browed monster for sending him off to do such demeaning work!

But then he remembered. He was only supposed to report good people. He gritted his teeth as they arrived at a half-built road. For twelve hours, he helped dig potholes and spread litter around. E.V.I.L. roads always got worse, not better.

"Well done, you've worked hard," said an older man in the team, clapping him on the back.

"Thanks," Otis puffed. It felt good to get

recognition for his efforts. Just in time, he remembered what he was there for and memorised the number on the man's ID badge. Employee 536 would be the first to be reported to Number 2.

He dozed through the return journey and hardly registered being collected and transferred to the S.H.O.E. orbiting above. Wearily, he ripped off his extra eyebrows and pressed the bracelet to summon Number 2.

"I'm listening."

Otis reported his findings. "He even led the singing on the way back," he said, remembering how everyone had cheered up when 536 had launched into song. "What will happen to him?"

The shrouded figure lifted her head. Otis just had time to see a faint, sinister smile before the screen darkened.

CHAPTER 3

False Ears
and Friends

Otis visited more planets after Drizz, and reported more people. It was astounding how many weren't mean and miserable, even though they had to work for E.V.I.L.

By the end of two weeks, he was tired. Tired of being undercover, tired of being new, tired of not being the most important person in the room. He wanted to go home. Failing that, he wanted the next workplace he visited to be filled with horrible people he didn't have to report. A gnawing, twisted feeling was tormenting him every time he

spoke to Number 2. As the transfer pod landed on Planet Slogg, he crossed his fingers and hoped for the worst.

"Have fun," Otis's bodyguard said, delivering him to the door of a warehouse signposted 'Product Adjustment Centre'.

Otis blinked with annoyance at the bright orange zunlight. Slogg was much closer to the Zun than Planet Vile.

"Don't forget your false ear," the bodyguard added, holding out a fleshy lump.

"Funny," Otis snapped. At the last planet, the crew had convinced him he had to wear an extra belly button. Hilarious.

"Suit yourself," the bodyguard said, smirking.

Otis scowled, stomped inside the building, saw someone with three ears and stomped back out again, snatching the appendage from the chuckling bodyguard.

"Hurray, another kid who doesn't know what they're doing," grunted the bored woman at the desk as he returned. "Here's your E.V.I.L. loyalty card."

Otis shoved the card with 'F.O.E: Friend of Evil' on it into his pocket with all the others. Good. It looked like this would be a pleasingly nasty place and he wouldn't need to report anyone. Number 2 wouldn't be happy, but at least he wouldn't get that horrible feeling, the one that made his eyes leak.

"Good morning!" said a bright voice.

A girl walked in behind him, his own age but different somehow, and it wasn't because her third ear was real. There was something about her eyes.

"Never going to respond, ever," grunted the supervisor. "Oh wait. Plob, Plub, whatever. Here's a new employee. I'm putting him on

lunchboxes. You're now on toasters. Make sure the bread pops in people's faces."

"Hi Plub," Otis said. "I'm O... liver." Oops. He had nearly self-busted by forgetting his cover name.

The girl grinned. "It's Plib. Sorry you've got to work here, Oliver, but you'll soon get used to the long hours, boring work and terrible pay. I'll show you around."

Uh-oh. That look. He had seen it in Employee 536: kindness. His eyes began to dart to the employee number on her badge. No, not yet. Maybe she'd turn out to be awful. Maybe there was still hope.

19

Plib took him on a tour of the warehouse, showing him how they were putting the finishing touches to products like the single-use lightbulb, the self-shredding umbrella and the slowly shrinking t-shirt. Otis was impressed, until Plib explained how customers were constantly forced to spend money they didn't have to replace the short-lived items. Somehow, the way Plib said it, it didn't sound so great after all.

"And this is you," she said, arriving at the lunchbox station and showing him how to preload the plastic boxes with mould. "Just shove the cheese in these cracks so they slowly start to stink. You'll get used to the pong."

It was the kindest sentence anyone had ever said to him. He felt his eyes doing that annoying thing with the water again and blinked them furiously. "Fine," he snapped.

She put a comforting hand on his shoulder. "It'll be okay. I know it all seems bleak and pointless, but you have to have hope."

He shook her off. He *had* to note down her number for that. Why wasn't he?

"But... long live E.V.I.L., right?" she added.

"Yeah," he mumbled. "Right."

The next twelve hours were spent handling mouldy cheese. He couldn't bear the feel, even through gloves, and did as little as possible. With any luck he would only need to last the day. During the single break, Plib introduced him to three other children who actually ate the awful lunch while chatting and joking. He couldn't understand why they were putting up with him until he realised: these were that thing he'd heard about called 'friends'. They were even sharing jokes with him about mending products instead of

ruining them like they were supposed to. At least, he hoped they were joking. He kept his head down so he didn't see their numbers. As soon as his shift finished, he rushed away.

"Get me out of here," he hissed to the bodyguard, and they hurried to where the pod was hidden in an alleyway.

Back at the S.H.O.E., Otis slumped in a seat and pressed the bracelet.

"I'm listening." Number 2's hooded face projected onto the wall.

Otis took a deep breath. "It's a totally evil E.V.I.L. workplace. So, er... no one to report."

"Not possible. Good people get everywhere. Like fleas. Wait a moment." Number 2 spoke into her own bracelet, then turned back to him. "Mrs Vile isn't happy."

"What's new?" Otis said daringly.

"I mean she isn't happy with you. You are

to stay at the warehouse until you've found good people to make miserable. Oh, and your ear looks stupid. I have to go."

The picture disappeared. Otis detached his ear and closed his eyes. Another day on Planet Slogg—but also another day of seeing Plib and her friends. Strangely, the prospect didn't feel as bad as he'd expected.

CHAPTER 4

Upsets and Uprisings

The next few days were the most enjoyable Otis could remember. He was even getting used to the harsh zunlight on Slogg. In fact, it made him feel good. And he actually looked forward to going into the Product Adjustment Centre with its bored supervisor and tedious, destructive work. He knew the reason. Instead of being taught by his grandmother to be E.V.I.L., he was being taught by Plib to be happy.

And what was so wrong with that?

Everything, of course. People weren't

supposed to be happy; they were supposed to spend money on worthless things to make his family richer. But Plib wasn't just a faceless consumer. She had a family she'd told him all about—a mum, dad and sister called Brox, who was a computer programmer. She liked animals and her favourite breakfast cereal was Fudgy Flakes. Plib was real.

And, with a flash of understanding, Otis grasped the awful truth: all the other people on all the other planets were real as well. They all had families and pets and things they loved. And they all deserved them just as much as he did.

He went into work that morning confused and distressed. He'd always known he was E.V.I.L. in big letters, but never thought about being evil in small letters. Until now.

That lunchtime, the atmosphere seemed

different. And not just because Plib and her friends were squeezing into a cupboard.

"You too, Oliver," Plib said.

Otis obeyed. He didn't want to miss out on having lunch with them, even if he didn't understand all the jokes, of which this was obviously one.

"Plib asked me to find a place we could meet in secret," Maxod said. He was long and red-haired and seemed especially friendly with Plib. Otis sidled past him begrudgingly.

"I have a... um... friend in the Resistance," Plib said in a low voice. "She programs computers and she has a virus."

"Is it the Splurts?" Arjax asked, pushing up his thick glasses. "I've heard that is really nasty."

Everyone laughed except Otis as he didn't know how. He would have to practise when he got back to the S.H.O.E. But he was also

shocked. Plib knew someone in the Resistance?

"A *computer* virus," Plib was explaining. "If we get it into the system, it will bring the whole warehouse to a halt."

"Why?" Arjax asked.

"Because someone has to stand up to E.V.I.L. Right?"

Otis felt himself go hot all over. He'd uncovered a plot! Surely this was the point where everybody would walk out and report Plib to the supervisor. *He* couldn't because he was undercover. But someone else would. Wouldn't they?

"This is just one tiny workplace," Arjax objected. "It won't make any difference. E.V.I.L. is on every planet in the Zolar System!"

"It will make a difference to us," Plib said.

Otis felt the sweat dripping off him.

Florn, another of Plib's friends, nodded.

"I'm sick of making life worse for people. Finally, we can do something!"

"Shh, they'll hear us!" Maxod said. "But I agree. I had to work here to get an E.V.I.L. loyalty card so my dad could get his disability benefits. It's not right. Arjax?"

"I too am sick of doing nothing. You're right, let's fight E.V.I.L. and the Vile family! But what about him?" Arjax pointed at Otis.

Everyone was staring at him. Otis wished he had more air.

"You can leave now and not be a part of this," Plib said gently.

Otis wanted to scream that he would tell, even if it did break his cover. But as he looked at Plib and the others and saw how they had put their trust in him, he realised he wasn't going to. And just like that, he had become a traitor.

"I'm in," he said shakily.

"Brilliant!" Florn said. "It's about time that old witch up there on Planet Vile got what's coming to her."

Otis choked so hard his ear nearly came off. They were calling his grandmother a witch! Unthinkable! But obviously they did think it. He wondered what else they thought.

"I hear her grandson's going to take over the company one day," he ventured.

"He's just as bad," Arjax said. "Apparently

Mrs Vile's son was alright. Until his mum slammed him into her own private dungeon."

"Lovely family," Florn said brightly. "Well, looks like we're all with you, Plib. But we haven't thought of the most important thing—a name."

Oliver's blood pounded away in two of his ears. The other one was barely hanging on. The words 'dad' and 'dungeon' were banging about inside his head until he felt sick. His dad had died when he was two—hadn't he?

"How about Gang of Organised Dissenters, or **G.O.O.D.?**" suggested Maxod.

Everyone agreed enthusiastically. Otis tried to nod without detaching his ear.

"Right, let's get some lunch—that stale bread and watery soup won't eat itself," Plib said. "Open the cupboard, Maxod."

Otis stepped out and gulped some air.

"Are you alright?" Plib asked.

"I'm fine," he lied, holding his ear on and stumbling away. He had to talk to Grandmother. Not via the bracelet, but in real life. He had to go home.

Number 2 didn't raise an eyebrow at his request, or if she did, he couldn't see it under her hood. "You still haven't given me any employee numbers from this warehouse, Otis," she said darkly.

"I will. Just get me back. I have to talk to Grandmother. Please!"

Number 2 disappeared. Otis thought his request had been ignored. But then he heard the ancient engines in the S.H.O.E. shudder into life. At last, he was on his way. But he wasn't the same Otis who had left Planet Vile.

Now he had a father.

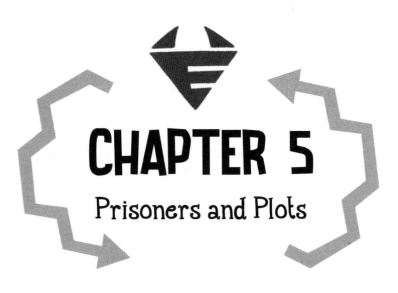

CHAPTER 5
Prisoners and Plots

"I'm disappointed in you, Otis."

Otis was back in his grandmother's office, facing her across the desk. This time he didn't want to be any closer.

"And I'm... I'm... disappointed in you!" Otis stuttered. It was hard trying to stand up to Mrs Vile, especially as he never had before.

"Such rudeness—I love it! Maybe the trip hasn't been a complete waste of time."

"Why didn't you tell me my father was alive?" he demanded.

"I never actually said he was dead. He was

fine before you were born, by the way. Chock-full of evil. But as soon as his little 'Otikins' appeared he went loopy. In 'love'. I should have known—nothing lasts."

"Where is he?" Otis asked in a small voice.

"There's a price for that information. One more number."

Otis shook his head.

"I'm getting close to fifty now. One more number and you can see your father."

"Why fifty? What's going to happen to them?"

Mrs Vile's eyes flicked to the window and the view of a massive cannon mounted on a rock.

"Oh no, you're going to fire them out of your giant space cannon, aren't you?"

"Whatever makes you say that?"

"Because that's what you do to people you don't like."

"True, but this time you're wrong. I'm going

to invite them to my Fifty Years of E.V.I.L. event. *Then* I'm going to fire them out of the giant space cannon. Oh come on, Otis. There must have been somebody you didn't like."

Otis thought back to the last time he saw Plib, joking around with Maxod.

"Yes. I suppose there was."

🌀

They walked to an unremarkable corridor where Mrs Vile unlocked an unremarkable door.

"Ten minutes. I'll send a guard if you haven't returned. We don't want you to get infected, do we?"

Otis opened his mouth to argue, but Mrs Vile was already walking away.

"Clock's ticking!" she called.

Otis galloped down a staircase and into a bare stone room.

"Father?" There was no answer. "Dad?"

"Is that... my Otis?" creaked a voice.

"Where are you?"

"Down here."

Otis crouched by a circular grating in the floor. An old, scruffy and very hairy version of himself in a ripped band t-shirt looked up at him from the rough cell beneath.

"Dad?"

"Otis! My son."

"Dad, I'm so sorry. I only just found out you were here. I'm so happy you're alive!"

"And I'm so happy you

found me! Did you grow up to be *very* evil?"

"I don't think so. Just a bit evil when I'm cross."

"Oh, everybody's like that. Talking of evil, did you hear the one about the evil shapeshifter? He turned himself into the police! Ha ha ha! Oh come on, I've got ten years of dad jokes to catch up on!"

"That's great, but we've only got four minutes."

"Oh dear. I'll just tell you the most important thing then."

"I know you love me, Dad. Grandmother told me."

"Oh. I was going to give you the code to your grandmother's computer so you could destroy E.V.I.L., but you're right, that would have been better."

"We've still got three minutes."

"You enter it on the keypad in her office. It's 1, 2, 3, 4. Can you remember that?"

"I did learn to count eventually, Dad."

"Good, because there's more. The keypad is giant-sized and each number must be held down at the same time by standing on it. So you need four friends who also oppose E.V.I.L. Can you do that?

"Er, yeeees," Otis said, feeling less sure. "Then what?"

"There's a big button saying 'Do you want to delete E.V.I.L.?'"

"Really?"

"No! That was another joke!" Dad rolled around on the floor with laughter.

"Very good, Dad, but what do I really do?"

Dad stood up and caught his breath. "Haven't a clue, son. That's as far as I got before your grandmother threw me in the

slammer. Now it's up to you."

⑥

"How was your father?" Mrs Vile asked, taking a helping of cremated duckling.

Otis faced her across the huge dining table. "He wants to destroy the company."

"Well I know, that's why I locked him away."

Otis slid a blackened wing onto his fork and forced it down. "The number I gave you before—that was false. But I see my duty now. There *are* more rebels on Slogg."

Mrs Vile leaned forward impatiently. "Their numbers, Otis!"

"You are going to invite them to the event, aren't you?"

"Yes, and then fire them out of the cannon. Quickly, boy! How many have you got for me?

With difficulty, Otis swallowed. "Four."

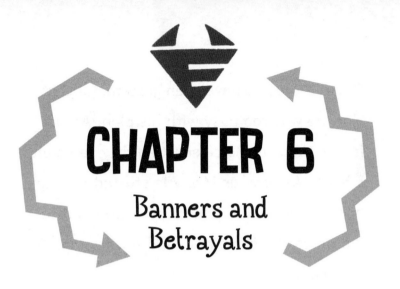

CHAPTER 6
Banners and Betrayals

Mrs Vile nodded with approval as Otis stood in front of her desk, dressed in the outfit she had chosen for him. "Perfect. I much prefer you in evil attire."

"These clothes aren't made by E.V.I.L. though, are they?" Otis asked, adjusting the collar of the supervillain-style cloak that matched his suit.

"Of course not. These gorgeous garments are made by my wonderful tailor over on Planet Lux. Only the best for the Viles."

Grandmother seemed almost... jaunty.

Once Otis would have been grateful for that. Now he was too busy with his plan. At last, it was the evening celebrating fifty years of E.V.I.L. As soon as Mrs Vile started making her speech, he would sneak off into her office, log on to the computer, and await help. *If* it came.

He took a deep breath. "Ready, Grandmother."

Just in time he remembered the door would lock behind them. He grabbed the first thing he touched in his pocket—an E.V.I.L. loyalty card—and placed it between the door and the frame as it closed. Mrs Vile was too jubilant to notice a thing.

The main conference hall was festooned with black and silver decorations. Baubles with Mrs Vile's face hung in bunches and a banner proclaiming, 'Fifty Horrendously Evil Years!' filled one wall. E.V.I.L.'s bestselling

products were showcased around the sides: the teeny tiny extra-losable remote control, the slowly fraying lift cable and, worst of all, the 90% air-filled crisp packet. In the centre was a scale model of the Zolar System onto which Mrs Vile had, over the years, slapped more and more letter Vs to denote the expansion of her empire.

"Mingle, Otis! Mingle!" Mrs Vile hissed as celebrities, who were here to be seen and knew it, and workers, who were here to be shot out of a cannon and didn't know it, drifted in.

Otis hated mingling. He had the feeling that most people didn't like him but had to be nice to him because of who he was. Instead, he looked for Plib. She wasn't here yet. Maybe she hadn't come? The thought made him both relieved and sad. She was the closest he had

ever come to having a friend—and yet he was putting her in terrible danger. He really was a bad person.

Just as he had reluctantly started telling some random VIPs about the scale model, he spied her: a slight figure in a puffy jacket and shabby dress.

"Oliver?" she gasped.

The cold presence of his grandmother fell across them like an icy hailstorm.

"I want you on stage with me, Otis."

"But—"

"But? But? Are you a goat, Otis? Now!"

"Right behind you, Grandmother!" Otis called, hurrying to Plib. Just seeing her gave him courage. But somehow she didn't look kind anymore. Now she looked like everyone else who hated him.

"You're a Vile?"

"It was the two ears that gave me away, wasn't it?" he joked nervously.

"No, it was the 'living on Planet Vile and calling Mrs Vile grandmother' that gave you away. How could you deceive us?"

"I was undercover. I'm sorry—"

"Sorry!? You betrayed us, didn't you? That's why we were invited here."

"No! I mean, yes, but there was a reason."

"I don't want anything to do with you."

Otis checked they weren't in earshot and lowered his voice. "1, 2, 3, 4 is the passcode for my grandmother's computer. I know you can do something. Your friends need to help too. Please, Plib—"

"OTIIIIIIIS!"

Mrs Vile screeched.

"I have to go. Her office is on Floor 66. Hurry!"

But Plib didn't move. All Otis could do now was join Mrs Vile on the stage where she was waiting to make her speech.

"Go on then! Introduce me!" she snapped, thrusting a sheet of paper into his hand.

Otis tapped the microphone. "Erm, wicked wishes to you all. Sorry, that's what it says here. Erm, may I introduce the woman who

44

taught the Zolar System how to consume like no one's consumed before. The founder and Chief Evil Officer of E.V.I.L., my grandmother Victavia Vile."

He stepped back, heavy with shame. Plib was still there. She obviously didn't trust him anymore. Well, he couldn't blame her. He *was* sharing the stage with the evilest woman in the Zolar System.

The polite applause died away as Mrs Vile spoke into the microphone. "Welcome, F.O.E.s, to this celebration of all things E.V.I.L...."

As Mrs Vile revelled in her success and everyone applauded except Plib, Otis could feel his pathetic plan turning to dust.

"But despite my efforts, there are still some 'nice' people around who 'want to make the world a better place'. I'm going to fire them tonight. Literally. The giant cannon has been

prepared and we will shortly be ejecting fifty specially selected workers from the group into the vacuum of space."

Otis saw Plib's face darken, and then she was gone. He closed his eyes. *Please*, he begged. *Please let it work.*

"But, before that, news of my successor. My grandson has recently been acting on my behalf, scouting the Zolar System for the enemies of E.V.I.L. And in this task he has completely... failed. Step forward, Otis."

Failed? Otis didn't understand.

"Come along. Show everyone what failure looks like."

With shaking legs, Otis moved forward.

"Despite all my efforts, you are still your father's son."

"But—I gave you the names..." Otis stuttered.

"Yes, and look at you. It's destroying you,

isn't it? So I have decided to disinherit you, just like I did him. My heir will be someone who is ever faithful, someone who has recently uncovered a rebel plot and delivered the culprits to my door—the wonderfully wicked Number 2!"

Everyone clapped dutifully as the hooded figure of Number 2 stepped onto the stage.

Who are *you?* Otis wondered for the millionth time.

Mrs Vile turned to the nearest security guard. "Take my ex-grandson to the dungeon."

CHAPTER 7
Statues and Sabotage

"This way," said the security guard, hustling Otis out of the hall. "Or is it this way?"

"We'll need the lift," Otis said, thinking fast.

The guard looked confused as they entered and Otis pressed Floor 66. "You can't have a dungeon on the top floor!"

"Have you ever been to Floor 66?"

"'Course not. That's the boss's floor."

"How do you know then?"

As Otis had hoped, the guard couldn't answer. When they got out, the single door to Mrs Vile's office was closed and wouldn't budge.

Otis shook his head sorrowfully. "I suppose it's because only the strongest guards can open it. Never mind—"

"Stand back!" The guard rammed the door with his shoulder. They burst in, forcing aside the desk which had barricaded it. Plib and her friends stood around four giant paving-slab-sized buttons next to a rolled-back rug.

"You found the access panel!" Otis said with a whoop. "Thanks for coming, everyone. Help me overpower this goon, will you?"

The guard, who was staring about him in shock, was swiftly jumped on by Maxod while Plib, Florn and Arjax tied him up with computer cables.

"The boss is going to kill me!" the guard moaned.

Otis ignored him. He couldn't believe it. Everybody was here—and they were helping him. "Thanks. For trusting me, I mean."

"Thanks for trusting *us*," Plib replied with a grin. "G.O.O.D. is back! Everyone, get on those buttons. Otis, we need you."

As Plib and the others stood on the buttons, a screen on the wall was uncovered and the words **'ENTER E.V.I.L.'** appeared on a glowing button. Otis selected it. Time to do some damage.

"Plib? Have you still got the computer virus?"

Plib emptied her pocket and looked at him, stricken. "It's not here. I don't understand. My sister should be here helping, but..."

"Don't worry, I've got a better idea. I'll start by disabling the cannon."

Otis had been trained thoroughly in the in-house computer system, clunkily named the System of Computer Knowledge or S.O.C.K. Swiftly, he found the right menu for the cannon and changed the slider to the 'off' position. There was a distant sound of powering down outside and a furious shriek, instantly drowned out by cheers from inside.

"Stay on those buttons!" Otis urged the others. "This is just the beginning."

"What else can you get into?" Plib asked.

"Cut the power?" Florn suggested.

Otis scrolled through the menus as fast as he could. "Good idea—if I cut it to the lower floors my dad will be able to escape from the dungeons. Done!"

"If your dad's free, will he be able to take over the company?" Plib asked.

"He's not evil enough for E.V.I.L., and neither

am I. I'll do as much damage as I can, then Dad and I will try to escape somewhere."

Otis felt a moment of giddy freedom. He didn't have to live with Grandmother anymore. He didn't have to be the Overlord of E.V.I.L. But where would he go? What would he do? His father would need looking after until he got used to his freedom.

"Come to Planet Slogg," Plib said, as though reading his mind. "It's zunny. And you can stay with us."

She couldn't mean it. Nobody could be that kind. "My grandmother won't be very happy with you."

"She won't be happy with me anyway after what we've done," Plib pointed out. "And we don't even know how we're going to escape so..."

"I can fix that." Otis pressed more keys.

"Right, the S.H.O.E. is ready for kick-off. I'll explain later," he added, seeing Plib's puzzled face. "Anything else we can do?"

"Ooh, ooh, ooh!" Arjax cried. "We should change their name! From E.V.I.L. to..."

"The Notable Industrial Company of Evil— or **N.I.C.E.!**" Maxod suggested. He was good at names.

"You could have given me a few more seconds," Arjax complained.

"Brilliant!" Otis said, actioning the name change. He had that soaring feeling again. Happiness. "Now, how can we make E.V.I.L. more N.I.C.E.? Let's start with working conditions. Free ice cream on Fridays, anyone?"

After a few minutes implementing some very interesting changes his grandmother would hate, Otis decided it was time they left. More guards would be looking for them

and they needed to get to the S.H.O.E. before Grandmother realised it was waiting for them.

"A thought," Maxod said. "What's to stop Mrs Vile undoing everything?"

"Hmm," Otis pondered. "Well, she hasn't got four friends, and the security guards don't come up here. I wonder how *she* unlocks the computer?"

"Does it matter? Let's get out of here before she does!" Florn urged them.

Otis helped Maxod and Arjax move the furniture back as new worries crowded his mind. What if this *had* all been for nothing?

Florn was looking at the replicas of Mrs Vile. "Those statues are truly awful."

"That's it! She must use the statues to weigh down the buttons!" Otis exclaimed. "But what can we do about them?"

"Well," Plib said, looking out of the window.

"It's a very long way down…"

As they came out of the office to summon the lift, brushing bits of statue dust off themselves, Otis saw someone waiting for him. His heart surged.

"Everyone, this is my dad."

"Pleased to meet you," Dad said. "Did you hear the one about—"

"Sorry, no time for dad jokes. Can we get to the S.H.O.E.?"

"We can try. Are these your friends?"

Otis looked round at Plib, Maxod, Arjax and Florn. "Yyyyes?" he said hesitantly.

"Of course we are!" Plib said. "Good to meet you, Mr Vile. You're very welcome to come back to Planet Slogg with us."

"Where Otis goes, I go," Dad said, smiling at him warmly. "But first, I quite fancy a ride in this device."

He pressed the button to call the lift. The doors slid open—and Number 2 stepped out.

"There you are, my little rebels."

CHAPTER 8

Breakdowns and Beginnings

They were so close to escaping.

"We're taking the S.H.O.E. and you can't stop us," Otis yelled.

"Stop us? She's coming with us!" Plib cried.

Plib had obviously never met Number 2.

The hooded figure didn't move. "I've got a job to do here. Something I've been working towards for a long time."

"You were planning to take over all along," Otis said bitterly.

To his amazement, Number 2 pressed the lift button and stood aside as the doors slid

open. "One day, I hope you'll understand. Now go on. Hurry!"

She was letting them leave? Plib looked upset as they entered the lift, but there was no time to ask her why. Otis pressed the Extra Fast button and they zoomed down to the underground hangar where the space shuttle waited, its lights blinking.

In the doorway stood Mrs Vile, her toughest security guard by her side.

"How lovely," she sneered. "My ex-family and some meddling underlings, trying to get away."

"Hello Mother," Dad said. "Do you know why mother kangaroos hate rainy days? Because the kids have to play inside!"

"I see you haven't changed, Ernold," Mrs Vile said witheringly. "Still acting like a pathetic teenager."

Dad grinned. "A pathetic teenager who once built his own spaceship! Come on, kids, let's take the cool car. This way!"

"Dad—what?" Otis panted as they all sprinted after him to a corner of the hangar.

Dad whipped off a tarpaulin. "I knocked this up when I was a youngster," he said with more than a hint of pride. "It may not be working after all these years, but..."

A few minutes later, they were streaking out of the hangar in a custom-made flying pod with go-faster stripes and fluffy dice in the window.

"This is so cool, Dad!" Otis enthused, taking in Dad's heavy metal posters and fantasy action figure collection as the others spread out on the multicoloured seats.

"Let's see if the communication system still works." Dad flipped a switch and the cabin filled with Mrs Vile's shrieks.

"Stop them, you useless lot! What's wrong with the engines? We should be using only the best quality parts from Planet Lux!"

Otis, Plib, Maxod, Florn and Arjax burst out laughing. They could hear Mrs Vile but she couldn't hear them.

"I think she's having trouble," Dad said as they watched the S.H.O.E. shakily lift into the

air, rise out of the hangar door a few feet, then drop to the ground.

"Sorry but there's been a supply chain issue, Mrs Vile. We've, um, we've been using E.V.I.L. parts for months now," said a hesitant voice.

There was an awful pause. "You're telling me we're using our *own* parts? Then this whole spaceship is a pile of junk! *Aaarrrrrgggggggghhhhhhh!*"

Mr Vile flipped the switch back off and replaced the noise of his mother with *Supersonic Meltdown* by Cosmic Death Lords. "Still got it," he said happily, settling at the controls as they zoomed towards Planet Slogg.

Otis grinned. Some things did last after all. Like home-built spaceships. And families.

"So you want to work on Planet Vile, eh?" said the man behind the desk at Slogg's local E.V.I.L. head office. "Where the action is!"

"That's right," Otis said, adjusting his glasses. They had clear lenses in but he was still getting used to them—and his hair, which was now blond. And his extra bio-arm, which Plib's mum had insisted on attaching so he wouldn't be recognised. "I've been working at the Product Adjustment Centre for a few weeks now but it just feels too... jolly."

"Jolly, eh?"

"Yes, ever since the new changes came in, the ones Mrs Vile announced were due to a computer error. It's such a warm and welcoming place. I mean, yuck! People shouldn't be enjoying work. Or cake. And the things they're making! Long-lasting,

creative products that enrich people's lives. It's sickening."

"Well, we do need more ambitious young people to rise in the ranks. And you sound like an ideal candidate. A real nasty piece of work! Here's your ticket for Planet Vile. Do your worst. Oh, and long live E.V.I.L."

It was hard leaving Plib, her family and his new friends, and even harder leaving his father, who was still recovering but planned to fight the system by becoming a subversive intergalactic stand-up comedian. But, as Otis boarded the shuttle heading into even more danger and uncertainty, he felt a strange kind of peace. There were two sides to every story, but now he knew which side he was on. And this time he wasn't alone.